RANDOM SHOTS IN THE JUNGLE

BY MR. S

Copyright © 2018

All rights reserved.

No part of this book may be reproduced or transmitted in any form or by any means, electronic or mechanical, including photocopying, recording, or by any information storage and retrieval system, without written permission from the publisher/author.

This is a work of fiction. Names, places, events and incidents are either the products of the author's imagination or used fictitiously. Any resemblance to actual persons, living or dead, or actual events is purely coincidental.

Cover design by M. Valerio

Hardcover ISBN: 978-1-9995079-2-3

Paperback ISBN: 978-1-9995079-1-6

Digital ISBN: 978-1-9995079-0-9

TABLE OF CONTENTS
PROLOGUE PROCLAMATION
Mirror Mirror…Who is the Greatest…

PART 1 – LOOKING OUT
1. Labels
2. Alliterative Life
3. Birthed for the Battle
4. Choices
5. Live the Dream
6. A Journey Part 1
7. A Journey Part 2
8. If I lost You
9. Expectations Lead to ...
10. My Fault
11. Insanity
12. The Damned
13. Boxes on the List
14. Change
15. Questions

PART II- LOOKING IN
16. My Golden Coffin with a View
17. Mind the Gap
18. The Wise Fool
19. Be
20. An Invisible Thread

EPILOGUE EPIPHANY

PROLOGUE PROCLAMATION

MIRROR MIRROR ...WHO IS THE GREATEST...

The greatest of all is felt but rarely seen.
There has never been or will ever be a comparison to thee.

You are the last moment of forever.

You're the beginning of history.

Many will try to be your equal.

That's mere delusional fantasy.

They need to know their place.

It's clearly well below you in existence's hierarchy.

The greatest of all is the foundation.
Many are ungrateful and unworthy of the world you create.

They think of themselves as advanced and free.

They're just sheep behind your gate.

Weak and starving because they have nothing to eat.
You nourish them with food on their plate.

The greatest of all is without competition.

While we trip over information with ignorance,

You're balanced on justice and wisdom.

Your words carry tremendous weight.

You are infinitely aware of all action.

Nothing is out of your power.

You are both problem and solution.

For, it is your will which sinks the sun.
Your commanding command refrain the rain.

Your soul shines the light in darkness.

Your spirit sparks hope's flame.
Creator of continents, countless kingdoms and civilizations,

Who is greatest of all, that over us all, will forever reign?

1

PART I - LOOKING OUT

This reflection found its origins near the end of the life of an unknown man. He lived at a time similar to now or in a not too distant past or perhaps in the not too distant future. The flow of his life served as valuable lessons to him, only revealed later in his life. In the beginning, like so many, his reflections combined to create a narrative rooted in the external. His retrospective lens focused on his interactions with his external world, which were a product of his decisions. The initial thoughts about his life centered around the purpose of things. To him, there was little point worrying about most things, including worrying. So many things he initially thought were important were eventually revealed as trivial in the grand scheme of life. He wasted a lot of his time trying to collect and keep things, especially the ones that his society deemed as proof of a great life. He realized that it was he who gave value to the things in his life. There was too much focus on the outside, titles and labels.

LABELS

Names only identify.

They never truly define.

Changing the labels of things doesn't make it something else.

The change is an illusion in your mind.

A lion doesn't become a cheetah because you add spots.
A zebra doesn't suddenly become a horse if you erase its lines.

It'll still graze and roam the land.

They're made all according to their intended design.

So quick we are to give multiple titles, describing basically the same thing.

We choose to sit on a bench, chair or an open seat.

Subtle difference doesn't change similar function.

We know a rose by another name still smells sweet.

It emanates its familiar fragrance to all it greets.

A new title doesn't change a man because he's promoted.

Societal status fluctuates with trends.

He'll be the same man when he's demoted.

A woman can grow from daughter to mother.

She's no different if you call her one or the other.

For, she'll never be father, son or brother.

What we are is who we are.
The titles we choose doesn't matter.

Calling another animal a cow

Won't make it any fatter.

Changing water's name doesn't make it wetter.

If I need relief from the cold,

Function doesn't change if it's called a hoodie, jumper or sweater.

It's not the name that keeps me warm in cold weather.

The same can be said of our relationships.
We have names like boyfriend, girlfriend, husband and wife.

All are different names for our partnerships.

Try to avoid the trappings of labelling things, a fruitless exercise.

It's like crying over spilled milk,

Resulting in wasted tears from your eyes.

2

He continues by describing the world in which he lives. It's a world seemingly created through the cultivation of contradiction. Where there was community there was also competition. Love and hate were locked in a perpetual battle, enhancing and destroying lives. Throughout his life he witnessed so many searching for their version of happiness in that horribly wonderful world. The shared struggle to secure satisfaction in life was the catalyst for his creation of a cryptic view of the world, as he saw it. So, he set about describing life.

ALLITERATIVE LIFE

Some seek society's secrets, sampling sparse, subjective satisfaction, sacrificing sanity. Searching for sustainable, suitable solutions sufficient to secure success saw so many stuck solving an indecipherable code. Cultures create catalysts carrying countless, coursing on a current of confusion.

The passage presumed to provide providence, paradoxically procured a plethora of permeating perspectives. Definitions deteriorate due to differing, deviant, delusional dispositions.

Haphazardly, hundreds hesitantly hope history hides the horrible human hostilities, harnessing hallucinations of happiness. However, hate hovers, holding hesitant hearts hostage.

Few fight for freedom from fear, forming firm foundations for a fortuitous future. Opposing, others opt out of obvious opportunities. Trust that time triumphs over the temporary truths transferred throughout this tactile terrain.

Change comes certainly. Rewards roam righteous roads, ripe and ready for receptive recipients. Why wait, why wander wherever? Walk willing where we must, without wondering why.

Let life lead, leaving lower levels laden with lies. Loathing labour, looking longingly, lost laughter, low luminescence? Life loses luster like lovers laying lamenting. Leave lethargy and live!

3

His thoughts then turned to his very beginnings, the moments of his first few breaths. That point in his life served as a reminder of potential not realized. All the tools he needed to have a prosperous life were given to him at birth. At that point, there wasn't anything he couldn't accomplish. Nothing could stand in his way. All he had to do was to cultivate his mind and body into a dynamic force for change and influence. However, he knew he wasn't the only one who promised so much, but along the way became lost. He knew he was foolish for not trusting is abilities and squandering his given gifts. So foolish he thought, because it was obvious to him now that he was more than prepared for life's endless battles.

BIRTHED FOR THE BATTLE

Birthed in the forge of the heavens
By an ancient god smith.
They created a living weapon.
Only a god could create this body I inhabit.

Given sculpted feet, swift with purpose.
They traverse any terrain.
How easily they adapt to any surface,
Ignorant to pain.

Given powerful legs delivering brute force,
Equaled by their agility,
They are filled with ferocity.
Victims of their carnage are plenty along its course.

They are topped by thunderous thighs thick and throbbing with terror.
They make the Earth tremble and quake.
When released, their power is felt over a great distance.
Even the rings of Saturn shake.

They injected a ferocious fire with a deafening roar.
It fuels my will and drives my focus,
Buzzing like a swarm of locusts,
Secured in the furnace of the most stable core.

The flames spark a fuse.
Fighting overwhelming energy giving my stallion heart life.
Its charge makes my fist crush mountains.
When opened and controlled, cut like a surgical knife.

They strike with absolute precision.
Against them there is no secure shield.
Surrender is the only option.
Even the most battle hardened, at my
hands yield.
If for some strange reason my enemies
persist,

Their pitiful attempts are easily brushed aside,
By the beams of steal above my wrists.
Only they are worthy to support my predatory pythons.
Monstrous arms powerfully packed,
If found within, squeezes the life from anyone.

They sit below broad strapping shoulders.
Combined with my bulging back,
The two make pebbles of boulders.
On them my most lethal component sits.
My head armed like a fighter jet,
Piloted by my computer like brain in its cockpit.
Targets identified through my radar eyes.
Their location confirmed aided by razor sharp hearing.
Where they hide this ultimate weapon finds.
Devastating defeat of all opposition is assured.
There's only one left standing,
When all others are floored.

4

Oh, the confidence and firm beliefs of youth, he thought. He remembered how unaware and sometimes uncaring he was about the consequences of his actions. He now had the time to assess his youthful exuberance. Childhood adventure after childhood adventure flashed through his thoughts. During those days of early life, he realized, were about discovery. The world was still new and his senses were constantly bombarded by new experiences. He was to use his sensory perspectives to connect the dots of life's tapestry. How was he to solve the riddle of his existence with so many distractions and choices?

CHOICES

It's either this way or another.

Any decision made,

Is fraught with trepidation and bother.

Senses given, rendered useless to me.

Five given abilities,

To understand purpose in this reality.

Together, constantly creating confusion,

Consistently questioning all of my beliefs.

When separated from each other,

Instantly revealed, is apparent dichotomy.

Ears allow me to hear so many sounds,

But, will I choose to listen?

Eyes allow me to see,
But will I choose to have a vision?

Body allows tactile experiences,

But will I choose to feel?

Tongue allows the sense of taste.

But will I choose to savor the meal?

Intoxicating fragrances inhaled by my nose.

Will I choose to just breathe and smell?

Choices cast me into clouded judgement,
Waywardly, aboard an empty vessel.

5

As he grew, the solution for his purpose and key to his true happiness was substituted with instant gratification. Self-control was a foreign idea to him. His desires became his driving force. He saw others and their constant hesitation to really go after what they truly wanted. Even at an early age, he knew he didn't want to fall into a similar trap. He was going to explore all that life had to offer. The goal at that point was to avoid living a life with regret. He was constantly regaled with stories of the almost and could have been and would have been. Charging forward, he wanted to live the dream.

LIVE THE DREAM

Why not give in to some temptations?
Must be a reason they're swirling in our heads.

Pleasure is a natural part of living.

Rejoice in the consequences or lament them when we're dead.

The impact of our actions is out of our control.

For even the best intentions,

Can be devastating to the whole.
Look no further than history's atrocities,

Stemming from proclaimed righteous goals.

Listen to conquers, liberators, or freedom fighters.

You'll hear different versions of the same story told.

There's no mystery why we fight each other.

We're always fighting ourselves.

No wonder why we lie to one another.

We start each day lying to ourselves.

Foolishly, placing our deepest desires,

Hidden, on inaccessible shelves.

We all get one life to live.

No one tells us for how long.

Will your story be one of fulfillment or
 One of wanting, like a sad song?

Time drifts by like hours of sleep,

As do we, enduring lives of regret.

At the end all we can do is reminisce,

About all that slipped through our nets.

If this is not the destiny you seek,

Find your own joy in each moment.

It's present in every second of every day of every week.

This is not as selfish as it seems.

Without happy, satisfied individuals,

You won't have a winning team.

Be free, let go and define your happiness.

Have more if the mood suits you.

Never settle for less.
Enjoy your private pleasures.

Don't be afraid to make a scene.

Moments don't wait forever.

WAKE UP!! It's time to live the dream.

6

Years of various memories of his physical and mentally development flashed during his recollection of his past. His lips began to curl upwards revealing a slight smile as he recalled past experiences. However, he realized that those memories provided further proof of his divergent course from the perceived norm. His approach and outward demeanor weren't aligned with common thought and practice. Again, he lacked belief in his ideology because it wasn't congruent with the masses. He fell into the trap of thinking he could find happiness outside of himself. He thought the search for love and happiness could be sought through others. During that time of his life, he was naive. He'd found pleasure in the company of many and thought that when he found "the one", they would be the key component for the acquisition of true happiness along life's journey.

A JOURNEY

PART 1

Permission not given to many, but the final destination worth every penny. Her seas hold untold treasures, including a glorious prize. So, I raise my sails and chart a course. My passionate adventure begins in the calm, inviting waters of her eyes. There's a quiet peace in their beauty. Their energy radiates like stars in the sky.

They draw me in and we become locked in a dreamy gaze. Deep within her stare lies the secrets to her body's maze. Now, nothing else matters and there's little left to be said. She seduces me into action and I lay her delicate body gently on the bed. Comfort created, casting off from the calm, I arrive at her lips.

Full of throbbing desire, they give life to broken, desperate ships. Time can lose all meaning to those who visit their shore. Temptation becomes stronger, I'm compelled to take a tour. I keep a thought in head as my will begins to fold. To complete my mission, I'll need to find something more valuable than gold. It's the virtue of self-control, the thing on which I'll need to hold.

Fortune favors the brave, so I follow her hip's lead. Independent thought vanishes and I do as I'm told. I succumb to the bounty that her sweet lips provide. They suddenly invite between them, revealing a moving sensation on which I glide. My body finds new life, filled with electricity. The feeling is so addictive. We become lost in ecstasy.

Luckily, this moment's true purpose magically crosses my mind. It's an arduous task finding release from her lip's enticing bind. Only she can release me from their powerful spell. Eventually, she sends me on my way with a loving gale. What other pleasures await me, only time will tell.

So, I venture forth, directed to the narrow straight of her neck. Suddenly, I begin to rise to attention. Her hands confirm my status with a stroking check. All her lips moisten at the thought of me being erect. She's excited by its power like a captain giving orders on deck. She teases me with up and down strokes, starting with a light and playful touch. She becomes lost in the moment. Her grip tightens as I grow and she sees how much.

I eventually refocus and engage in a slow meander along her neck's sensitive trail. Giving sudden risings of her levels, every touch registers with heart racing detail. I navigate the undulating movements of her body's tides, on a course from neck to ear. Water temperatures begin to boil. Elevated emotions make it difficult to steer.

Our movements attempt to become one. Again, my ultimate goal is lost, at the back of my mind, forgotten. I'm adrift on her tactile flow. Every breath felt on her neck is greeted with sighs of, "Yes". I await more commands to follow. Her moans of, "Yes", turn into pleas of, "Lower, lower." All her ports are starting to open up and I have so much to show her.

As I continue my amorous quest, I find myself amidst a valley, between two perfectly sculpted breasts. It's like being caught between divine glory and beauty's true magnificence. Slowly, tenderly, I climb to their peaks. With a hand I sensually caress one. The other clenched ever so slightly between my teeth. A shiver runs throughout her body, ending with uncontrolled convulsions of her feet. Deep desires are rising, about to burst at her surface. There's a rush of heat and uncontrolled motion. In her body's storm, twin peaks give me safe purchase.

Her unconscious, erotic gyrations give me a sign. Things are moving in the right direction. They're integral to my adventure's design. The waves of her body send me away from her valley of bliss. The current sends me to her trembling core. Writhing, craving and anticipating because she's in an orgasmic crisis. She wants to erupt like never before. Her words begin to echo, "More, more, more!"

My tongue surfs the coast near her most sensitive region. It's her most treasured harbour. It's a place that allows our bodies to join in symbiotic fusion. Her body rises and crashes like waves, driven by sensations colliding. There's a distant glint of her hips on my horizon.

7

Sensual pleasures and past lovers bouncing around his mind gave rise to a sudden pause. During the contemplation of the multiple potential partners that he had amorous interactions with, he realized that, at times, he became lost on his journey. He allowed pleasures of the flesh to blind him from the reality of his circumstances. However, it was a necessary part of his journey and it made him realize that it provided a learning opportunity. He was lucky to find companionship and even the most twisted version of love was better than having none. It wasn't about the destination, because real learning was derived from the continuation of his journey.

A JOURNEY

PART 2

Her hips invite me closer, as they turn and twist. Temperatures inside are near maximum. My tongue makes a moist yet tender visit. A slow, stimulating, sensual course lifts her midsection to the sky. Her body's moisture glistens in the light. I make my way teasingly along her inner thigh.

Without warning her legs open wide. My final destination's now within sight. My mind drifts to salacious intentions of being inside. Conditions are perfect and she seems ready. Her craving for carnal pleasures, she cannot hide. I've come so far and enjoyed my time. Why rush now, the sudden thought in my mind. A few more moments of intimate discovery will suit us just fine. Her harbor will be even more inviting when I return down the line.

So, I carry on weaving a captivating course. Moisture's now freely flowing. Her swollen engorged harbour the source. Those waters lead me to the back of her knee. It's a hidden cove laden with sensitivity. She's primed to explode at the next slightest touch. Her body's crying for release so much.

Every fiber of her being bursting at the seams with unreleased passion. Crafted calves lead to her the end of her seas. I circumnavigate fragile feet encased in high end fashion. So often they're overlooked because of their distance from her harbour's prize. However, they're no less sensual, judging by the roll of her eyes.

There's a little-known secret about feet. They're connected to all erotic zones. She feels them as I engage each one. I start at her sole and finish at her toes. This isn't the end because there's one place left. I n e e d to find her colour flushed, rich harbour. It's the true purpose of my coupling quest.

So, I retrace the steps of this erotic odyssey. Only this time, it's done with more urgency. She won't last much longer. Her trapped passion needs to be set free. The path to her freedom is steady and straight. It leads to her divine harbour that calls to me.

Before entering her moist entrance, a spot above requires attention. It's a most sensitive area, requiring a coded touch. All defences dissolve as I unlock its secrets. Slowly I enter while she secures me between her legs' clutch. This pleasurable passage is kept hidden, a secret from most. Its trail opened to me and designed by a delicious host.

Two are now one after I enter. My voyage so close to completion as I weigh anchor at her center. The end comes when we reach mutual release. Dual orgasmic climax erupts from deep within. Our bodies lay limp, rational thoughts cease. Indescribable feelings coursing through both of us. This our shared journey, so wondrous.

8

The journey was teaching him so much, but sometimes, he wasn't paying attention. Even from an early age, he recognized the power of his emotions to take control. They had the ability to cloud his judgement. So difficult to control and even in his final days, he never achieved the mastering of his emotions. His heart had the power to defeat his mind. Logic would help him turn the tide in the battle between feelings and facts. However, the heart was a cunning foe who waited for the perfect time to strike. Whenever he grew attached to someone, anxiety about their loss in his life would sometimes overwhelm him. This would include his wife, children and cherished family members. So many times, he confessed to himself and his past loves, "I wouldn't know what to do, if I lost you!"

IF I LOST YOU

If I lost you,
Life is an empty thing.

If I lost you,

I'm lost in darkness where your light is missing.

If I lost you,

I'm like a bee without its sting.

If I lost you,

I can't hear the sound of my heart beating.

If I lost you,
Life isn't worth living.

If I lost you,

I'm lost in space, aimlessly drifting.

If I lost you,

I'm like a shark without its fin.

If I lost you,

I can't breathe because I'm suffocating.

If I lost you,
Life loses all meaning.

If I lost you,

I'm lost at sea, hopelessly sinking.

If I lost you,

I'm like an eagle without its wing.

If I lost you,

I can't see a reason to live because I've lost everything.

9

Instead of learning to let go, he was growing attached to the material world, including a list of lovers and those he deemed important in his life. In that moment of thought, a connection was made. His attachment had only served to increase his insecurity. So much, he thought he had to lose. Remembering how he tried to hold on to things out of his control, made him realize that he was creating unrealistic expectations. They were only going to guide him on a wayward path void of satisfaction. For, having expectations of things and people that are truly out of one's control only leads to ...

EXPECTATIONS LEAD TO...

You expected complex thought.

From a simple mind this was sought.

Ask a dog trained to seek and find,

To guide someone who's blind.

All involved become distraught.

When you thought it's clear and evident,

Realize, only you knew what it meant.

Don't expect me to always understand.

Babe, I'm just a simple man.

This will only lead to an argument.

So, remember my love!
If you think it's obvious and true.

Lower your expectations,

Which lead to disappointment,
It's complex for me when it's simple for you.

10

There was an obvious conclusion to all his misery. He realized that he was never forced to submit to the will of others. He made those decisions on his own. Thinking it was good to put others before himself only revealed the nature of others. Many were ready and willing to take advantage of kindness. They weren't thinking of the balance of give and take. However, there was only one person to blame. Upon an honest reflection it became clear, the fault was his.

MY FAULT

Forgive this simple creature.
I keep forgetting I'm to blame.

Everything that happened, it's my fault.

I didn't remember it's all about you. I didn't remember it's not about me.

I forgot, it's my fault.

I made you lose your way. I should get lost.

Having no direction, it's my fault.

I turned your dreams into a real nightmare.

Reality, it's my fault.

You made your bed but I made you sleep in it.

Sleepless nights, it's my fault.

You wanted so much but I only gave you what you need.

No satisfaction, it's my fault.

I tried to lead but you refuse to follow.

No guidance, it's my fault.

You wanted control but I stood my ground.

No power, it's my fault.

Your hunger for even more was evident but I didn't make you eat.

Starving, it's my fault.

When your pride made you fall, I didn't catch you.

Hubris, it's my fault.

So, I try to get you to your feet but you don't want my help.

No support, it's my fault.

You prefer to struggle even though I have a solution.

The obvious conclusion is it's my fault.

If I'm lucky enough to be asked questions, you don't want my answers.

No solution, it's my fault.

When I try to simplify you say it's complicated.

No comprehension, it's my fault.

You're deaf to sound advice because I don't understand.

So blind to the fact, it's my fault.

Maybe I should try to get closer but I'm kept at a distance.

No connection, it's my fault.

I don't understand your actions. So, I make my own story.

The narrative created, it's my fault.

I'm dammed if I do and I'm dammed if I don't.

Either way, when it's all said and done, it's my fault.

It's difficult to accept this but without acceptance, it truly is my fault

11

Darkness rose noticeably at that point of his memories. He was constantly fighting himself and societal norms. It was a time that allowed the unchallenged assault on his character, ideals and his will. Knowing the outcome of the battle, gave him some comfort. He allowed his beliefs to be weighed against the legitimacy of the prescribed system. His thoughts spiraled beyond his intentions and he only found inconsistency. The mental search for clarity almost led him down a road of insanity.

INSANITY

Am I sane, living in an insane world, or am I insane, living in a sane world?

It's a delusional dream of a common-sense merchant applying his trade in an economy of emotional reasoning. Customers for my merchandise are clear and presently preoccupied with my competition, who promise happiness through the accumulation of material quantity in the market place.

They are motivated by illusions created by an unknown master. I try to be of value but I have no equity. My trinkets of truth just don't appeal to the blind, potential client. Even pearls of wisdom, given freely, aren't of any interest to emotional fools. My hidden gems that create a sense of wonder and awe continue to lay in open secret, overlooked by ignorant consumers. They crave false value stocks of external distraction. What the few possess, the majority seek.

Eventually they learn it's a portfolio overflowing with fool's gold. Then, they place the blame and the resulting emptiness of their fortune on the unfortunate. So, convinced it's not their fault even though familiar foreboding misfortune awaits all who ignore painful truths, like the buyer should always beware. If only they could turn back time and invest in a more successful currency.

I would've advised the pursuit of peace of mind, which is priceless. However, time cannot be bought or bargained with. Consequently, all their efforts to acquire control only results in a bankrupt state, void of morality, spirituality and satisfaction. The keys to their success are within their grasp but remain elusive. Their hands are bound by their lack of courage to face life's challenges.

I advertise logic as the mechanism for their release, but my intended demographic boycotts my campaign. They rally to the cause of representatives who perpetuate their fears. Although I petition for change, so many may prosper, I'm outvoted by those who want to keep the status quo. Thus, the cycle of hypocrisy and contradiction continues to fuel the current system.

Now, a person's word has decreased in value and their actions lack responsibility. Talking the talk is the accepted and proof by walking the walk is rejected. It's given impetus from the equal and easy access to information thus creating a network of refocused faith. As the unknown loses its mystery, there suddenly is a rise in man-made crops of perceived insight.

The process of pain staking research and study through higher learning is no longer required. Critical thinking and objective analysis succumb to the immediate gratification of a search engine. The engine that galvanizes our ingenuity is stifled. Creativity cannot breathe without initiative. Instead of building on an illustrious past, regurgitation has taken hold.

We subscribe to sequels and prequels to sedate our adventurous spirit. Luckily, there's the enduring concept of hope. It is hope which pushes us forward even though some want to go back. It seems crazy to have hope in a world so far gone. Maybe I'm crazy for giving up hope in a world that has come so far. The realization concluded from such thoughts and using logic to make sense of this illogical life, is a chronic condition of insanity.

12

He remembered how low his world became at some points. In those moments, many choices were resigned down to two. Honestly, he remembered how the decision between the two nearly tore him apart. The choice of giving up was gaining momentum on the alternate proposition. The other choice was more difficult than cashing in his chips. His character shone through in those difficult moments and an overwhelming sense of pride grew inside of him. Pain and suffering were a natural part of the living experience and he was supposed to have his share. Somehow, he found the strength to keep fighting. His initial given powers he'd learn to forsake, returned to his very being. He was born ready, fell asleep and now awoken. The damned fool, dare not quit!

THE DAMNED

Keep fighting you damned fool.

Don't you dare quit.

The road may be muddy.
It may be filthy deep and thick.

Keep fighting you damned fool.

Don't you dare quit.

The path may be long and winding.

There may be no end to it.

Keep fighting you damned fool.

Don't you dare quit.

The doors may be closed.
It may be the same at every visit.

Keep fighting you damned fool.

Don't you dare quit.

Your fall may feel like a plunge into a well of despair.

It may feel like a bottomless pit.

Keep fighting you damned fool.

Don't you dare quit.

The time may come for you to lead.

It may feel like some try to resist.

Keep fighting you damned fool.

Don't you dare quit.

You may feel like you can't move forward.
You may feel the urge to give up and sit.
Keep fighting you damned fool.
Don't you dare quit.

You may feel like you don't have enough to persevere.
It may feel like a huge deficit.
Keep fighting you damned fool.
Don't you dare quit.

This race is for those who can endure, not the quick.
Refuse until your dying breath to quit.
Keep fighting you damned fool!

13

Of all his achievements of his life, he was most proud of those moments when he refused to quit. Life provided many instances of telling blows, finding their mark, knocking him down. None were more painful than the emotional trauma of separated love. Pain, disappointment and loss were not exclusive to him. Everyone was well aware of their influence and the opportunity they provided for learning and growth. As part of his growth, was his increased ability to find answers through his personal logic, which often sought connections. He connected that his current, past and future circumstances were chiefly of his own making. It was he who concocted his misery through setting unrealistic expectations and applying them to reality. So, each time he fell, he knew he played his part. After, he was equally, if not most, responsible for his rise from the ashes of his destructive fires. The pattern of periodic renaissance increased his self-belief. He became less afraid to not conform with popular thought. He started to ignore the labels which were often misleading. There was the abandonment of the irrational search based on unwarranted expectations. Humans were not perfect and shouldn't be expected to tick all the boxes on his list.

BOXES ON A LIST

You continue to search for someone,

To tick all the boxes on your list.

There'll be no compromise for available suitors.
None seem to meet your requirements, yet you'll persist.

Crying to the heavens, you desperately pray.

Hopefully, your petition will be answered.

Hopelessly, you wait for that faithful day.

Looking longingly, you see others who found their mate.

It feels unfair that they're rewarded.

While, misery seems to be your fate.

They found a worthy candidate for their boxes.

To you it's a mystery.

All you seem to attract are oafs and clumsy oxen.

Some uncovered the secret to find their fish in the sea.

While others found their needle in haystack,

You only discovered a way to be lonely.

Maybe they didn't have a list.
Maybe they tried to give of themselves, not looking to receive.

Maybe they wanted to satisfy another.

Maybe they chose to be honest, not looking to deceive.

Maybe they entered with pure intentions.

Maybe you're in a box, unable to breathe.

Maybe, your list has blinded you.

The loneliness is suffocating and you're unable to see.

Perfection is what we strive for.
It's an ideal we'll never achieve.

Stop looking for boxes of love.

True love fits like a glove.

Love finds you when the time is right, magically.

14

He recalls that during those moments of clarity, a feeling of intangible growth occurred. At least, that's what he thought. However, his odyssey through time and tactile space made him realize that there was a cyclical nature to things. Perspectives and perceptions change only to return at some later point. Therefore, logically, he was changing only to return to his former self. That moment and train of thought was difficult to comprehend. If that were true, then his childish mind was more intelligent and powerful than he had previously realized. To compound his cognitive dissonance was the realization that logic was tough to beat. Moments from his childhood, which provided proof of this were suddenly vivid in his mind. There were moments, where through the eyes of a child, wisdom of action was easily found. As a child, situations were simplified, while adults muddled in complication and/or complexity. More supporting evidence of the cycle revealed itself by remembering about his birth. He was born consciously knowing nothing of his world and upon his exit he knew he was as equally ignorant as his infantile self. Was there any change at all?

CHANGE

Funny how change comes with time.

All wounds, time is supposed to fix.

However, time has some issues.

Some say time doesn't exist.

It's ebbs and flows,

Others can't resist.

Does it have an equal?

What's its antithesis?

Can it ever be controlled?

Why is it like water, constantly slipping through my fists?

Oh, you with no beginning or end.

Time, you give more than enough.

However, when times are tough,

You're definitely not my friend.

Why do you always play it safe,

Never a twist or turn?

With you comes endless obstacles.

Why do I never have enough of you to burn?

I hope you're enjoying your sick game.
Watching creatures of habit trying to learn and change,
Knowing damn well, like you, we'll just stay the same.

15

To him there was a change, recognized or not. Looking back, he realized that the most important change he had to make was a change of focus. Although an external view provided some insight, he still needed to venture deeper. Instead of creating increased clarity, the external view seemed to generate more questions than answers. Variations of philosophical questions flooded his thoughts. Could his logic provide the solutions? He had reached a point in his life that allowed time for prolonged reflection. He recorded some of his most pressing questions and took some time to contemplate the answers.

QUESTIONS

Who's right and who's wrong?
Is there a difference between lies and truth?

Does the answer come with seasoned age?

Can it be found in impetuous youth?

Why aren't our perspectives aligned?

Are we really that different?

Will someone please show me a sign?

Shouldn't we come together?

Isn't that the wise choice?

Wouldn't we be better off?

Could we unite in one voice?

Where is it written for us to separate?

When did we decide this is our fate?

Has it worked so far?

Did it serve us well?

Will we ever change?

How can we break this spell?

What is it going to take?

Do we know what's at stake?

There's no wrong or right.
The difference between the truth and fiction
Will always come to light.

Some answers are revealed through seasonal change.
Others were evident from the beginning,
Even at an early stage.

From the moment we opened our eyes,
We found ways to remain blind.
Ignoring all warnings signs,
We aimlessly search for what we can't find.

Only by working for the whole,
Will we find peace.
Singular ambitions lead to destruction,
Allowing suffering to increase.

We have the choice to be better than before,
If we stand together as one,
Then prosperity is assured.
We have the power to calm turbulent shores,
Fly where eagles soar.
When we commit to this,
We're prepared for what the future has in store.

PART II - LOOKING IN

He had dissected his life, but he knew it was from a singular perspective. The external examination consistently led him back to his obligation of looking at himself. Subscribing to his logic and if his life was primarily of his making, he needed to investigate the source. So, he surrendered to an honest self- assessment. There would be no point trying to deceive himself. He would be lying to himself, which he thought was the worst lie of all. How ridiculous was it, to be dishonest with the only individual totally aware of your intentions and personal history, yourself? So, he began his voyage into the depths of his consciousness and started to look in.

16

MY GOLDEN COFFIN WITH A VIEW

I've yet to discover a purpose for the pointless promises, arbitrary arguments and counterproductive conversations over the years. Some of the worse have involved the people I thought I knew. The result is my friendship circle being quite small. It's a tight, valuable ring of just a few. I've had way too many interactions with sheeple who, are never at fault for their own misery and doom. The blame for their painful life experiences is usually placed externally, perpetually creating excuse after excuse.

I keep hearing, "It's not my fault, you don't understand."

They continue to, list all the reasons why things didn't work out. The only reason I see, is they didn't have a vision or a plan. I will never claim to have all the answers. Forgive me, if I've ever claimed to be a smart man.

Apologies, but I've realized that you need to pay attention to life's lessons. In their teachings there are many things to know. For example, if you fail to prepare, prepare to fail. Many refuse to heed this warning tale. Yet, they're surprised how their life goes.

Usually, I end up at odds with these people. There are so many instances I could organize them in row after row. I could continue, and go on until my face turns blue. No one has the patience for that. So, I'll share some examples of what I've been through.

I remember when I was very young my father used to say, "You're my son and I love you. You're a part of me and I will always be there for you!" He says the same thing when we occasionally see each other, even to this day. In the beginning, his words gave me comfort. I felt we were forever bound. However, as I grew from child to adult, somehow, he was never around. What's been needed to fill his absence in my life has never been found. It's probably my fault. I still haven't made my father proud. I guess absence makes the heart grow fonder. Maybe that's why we're rarely in the same town, let alone the same crowd.

Before you start getting emotional or wasting tears from your eyes, I want you to know that it's not all bad. The balance of the universe blessed me with one of the greatest parents history's ever had. It's just my humble opinion, but I'm so amazed. From humble beginnings, she accomplished so much, with next to no support, being both mother and dad. She committed to the role of parent with unrivaled energy. To her it wasn't a game or passing fad.

She's a blessing in my life. Trying to make a better life for us two, she did what she thought was best. I love her, but she's not perfect. She's played her part in this living mess. Helping me to survive and prosper in this world, so many things on me, she tried to impress.

Try as she may, with all the power she had, time after time she would say, "You need to stay away from drugs, nothing good comes from them, only bad. They'll drive you insane and ruin your life. Think of all trouble with drugs this family has always had. Remember your cousin who was doing so well in school until he got caught up all those drugs? Well, now he's a homeless bum on the street, out of his mind, totally mad!"

The first time she warned me, I didn't question her, and said, "Mom, you're right and thanks for reminding me…I'm glad. There's no way I'm gonna end up like him, with all his issues. Drugs are only gonna make my life sad."

Like a good boy, I did what my mother told me to do. Eventually, over time, rebellion began to poke its fiendish head through.

It was the catalyst, for me to start to give in to. So, along the way I experimented with a drug or two. They included two of the most dangerous, but somehow legal, cancerous cigarettes and infamous booze. They quietly became part of some of the best times I ever knew. Strange how the things people feel are negative, can sometimes feel like a positive. I was beginning to wonder if anyone knew the correct way to live. Surely drugs weren't responsible for so many people taking without an inkling to give.

Strangely, when I think about it, I also take. I was taking classes in school during the weekdays for quite some time, with a guaranteed two-month break. My school teachers also contributed to nonsense with the things they used to say. They seem to regurgitate the same line, "Focus on your work. Later, you'll have time to play!"

Other teachers tried to motivate me with the typical catch phrases. I would hear it in room after room. Stop me if you've heard this one, "Aim for the stars and if you miss, at least you'll hit the moon."

I got in trouble when I decided to blurt out a response to that profound point of view. It got me a one-way ticket to an hour's detention that same afternoon. With cheek and a hint of sarcasm, at him I let loose, "Sir, I can't reach the stars or the moon. They sound like awesome places, but I'll die right away. I won't be able to breathe, but man, what a view!"

The pointless mess would continue. I wasn't the best player on any of my Catholic high-school basketball teams. Some of the best thought they were destined for the NBA.

I asked some of those the same set of questions, "How much do you need to practice to make it all the way? Is it 24/7? Is it day and night, Monday to Sunday?"

Their responses increase the shaking of my head, each time they replay. Shrugging his shoulders, one would say, "I'm already pretty good. Plus, everyone thinks I'm going to make it anyway! I'll just keep doing what I'm doing and with a bit of luck and a lot of prayers, bro, pray...."

He paused, looked to the heavens, then continued, "Pray, pray, pray!"

With bewilderment I listened to another say, "I ain't got all that time for practice, got other stuff going on. You don't understand, with your perfect life, ain't got time to play!"

After, try as I may. Every question with which I countered, seemed to only create dismay. They included, "You mean to tell me, all I need is prayer to change my grades into A's?"

"Why did I waste time studying for my test today?"

"Are you sure all I need is luck to be the best, without practice?"
"All I need is what I learned yesterday?"

"Bro, why are we even in school then? When the coast is clear, let's make a break!"

In the end, consistently I encouraged them to drop without delay. That was a chapter of my life that was suddenly over. Then, I really got tossed into the fray. So, I began to work and date more in my adult days. I began to realize people didn't progress past their childhood ways.

I was seeing this chick who ticked a lot of my boxes. She was hot and fiercely independent, possible the "one"! However, she kept saying, "I like to do things on my own. There's nobody I need to depend on. I got my own stuff and don't need anything from anyone, especially no man!"

In response, I asked, "What are you doing with me then? How do I fit into your no man plan?"
She replied, "You don't get that I love you, silly! Don't you understand?"

Strangely, it didn't work between us and she got her wish. The sea became empty and she's the only fish. When people say they are so independent, it's because they don't want to commit. They think it shows strength of character but, it's just a myth. Instead of giving up a little independence, so many would rather quit. It's just sad when people try to convince me, with all their bullshit!

I've dated many potential suitors to try find my match, my boo. It became a cycle of the same old, same old, nothing new. For example, in an intimate relationship, during a conversation, while staring into my partner's eyes which were sparkling blue, I said, "Babe, there's no point in us trying to be rich!"

She said, "That's not true!"

Without hesitation, she continued, "All we have to do, is use our energies to work hard, save, invest wisely and we'll be prosperous too."

Then I commented, "Where are we going to put all our stuff when we die. Anything we buy, won't remain shiny and new."

We eventually went our separate ways and bid each other adieu. Then there were a lot of exes who used to say the same old line, "You're lucky I cooked for you. I don't do this for just anyone."

I became less surprised to hear it. Their words felt like an ultimatum. So, I told the same thing to every single one, "Someone cooking for me is not something I depend on! It's a good thing I can cook for myself. Don't worry about future meals for me from your spice rack and shelf."

Another potential life partner had money and influence. After one of our initial dates, she preplanned our future in just one afternoon. She told me, "When we are married, you'll be rich and hopefully soon. We'll be smart and invest in a large luxurious house. Ooh, I can't wait to redecorate every single room."
Then, there was my wife who promised 'til death do us part. I guess she tried to speed up the process when she tried so many times to rip out my heart. She left, took the kids and the house, pretty much everything. There was nothing left but emptiness in my marriage cart. Somehow, I knew, I felt it from the start. We

would eventually go our separate ways, destined to be apart. So, again I became the fool, when I should've played it smart. It's just another example of life imitating art. The cycle I was trying to break continued, all according to my life's chart.

There were those people at work, who I realized, didn't have a clue. I asked one, "How can I find more time for friends and family?"

With a wink and a smirk, he replied with his sly tune, "Who has time for all those people? I somehow missed most of my reunions, especially the ones in June."

I complimented a colleague on their bling, which they said was a way to accent their wealth. Cheekily, I responded, "I choose to accent my partner's life as a loving groom."

He laughed and mockingly answered, "What the hell does that mean? You're doomed but good luck with no freedom in your life. You'll be even more tied down with children. Be like me and cut them out with an unemotional knife. I bet you're looking at me, living the dream, wishing you could have just one of my beautiful rides. Soon, you're gonna beg to trade your family including your kids and especially your wife! You're dumb bro, you have so much to learn!"

He probably thinks he's going to be cruising in the afterlife on a yacht. He'll be the same one crying, begging for life, when Death says, "It's your turn!"

So many people concerned with money and wealth. They always pretend they don't want other people's money. Just like a recently divorced friend who told me, "In the beginning, everything was roses, things were sunny. I wasn't looking for his cash. I really loved my husband, my honey."

I started to laugh and say, "You're hilarious, so damned funny!"

Getting upset she replied, "What do you mean? I really loved that dummy! I really don't get whey you're laughing. I can still feel the pain deep in my tummy."

So, I explained, "You claimed you loved him and it wasn't about the money. But when it was over, you fought so hard for half of his stuff and a substantial financial pay-out during alimony."

Her complaints ended quickly like some of my career pathways. I tell you a few of them from past days. Some bosses tried to correct my perceptions. Others constantly tried to show me the error of my ways. A boss I had, once told me, "Son, when you took that week off to go surfing waves on that secluded beach, you really missed a chance to maximize your sales and increase your pay. If you want to get ahead, you gotta be in the office, gotta slave for profit in every way. Instead of being like everyone here, you're wasting your life away. You should live to work not work to live. Focus on paying your dues to the company every single day. Taking a wintery weekend to go up to the cottage is just dumb and a waste. Who wants that fresh, alpine powder in your face, anyway? Instead, you gotta grind, even if it's away from home. Buried deep in paperwork, not sand, will pay off one day!"

I continued to clash with his philosophy and was subsequently let go, after a couple of months, ending in May. So, I tried to start my own business to beat the rat-race. It's difficult on your own. I took a partner who thought he was successful and he used to say, "You could be like me, in a better place. Follow my lead and you'll be rich for life and even in death!"

I told him, "Don't hold your breath! If that means spending sleepless nights working, spending time away from friends, family and my home base, I choose to be poor and alive, chilling in a hammock, with a cool breeze dancing in my face."

His face grew in frustration. He was surprised and annoyed, because he couldn't believe I was defending my case. These people's frustrations always seemed to turn into anger. They're consistently letting me know their feelings and deeply their pain is felt. At times, I ask them, "Where are your emotional bruises? Where is the emotional welt?"

I would continue to blast my so-called friends, "Material possessions are not paramount, especially not over your health. If you become very ill, you won't be able to enjoy all that wealth."

The arguments seem to rage on and on, everyone gets increasingly vexed. Both sides professing to be right and the other 100% incorrect. Sometimes, I engaged in conversation with non-empathetic, cutting people who have said, "The poor will always be miserable in this life and the next."

"If you're rich in life, it's the same in death."

Is eternal pleasure only reserved for those who are the richest? When they pass, I won't be among the visiting guests. I won't have a change of attitude. My living, beating heart won't let me apologize to them. I won't be on bended knee, repenting the servitude.

So many persisted because of my perceived lack of faith in their system. For, I tended to question what they thought they knew. Unresolved, we tended to split with parting random shots fired. The frequency would increase as the distance between our worlds grew. All that was left, was a bridge of tension between us two. I've played my part in this ridiculousness. I've been guilty of ignorance since way back when. I'll finish with a childhood altercation. It was with a classmate when I was around ten. Somehow, I felt he was being unfair in the battle of who was going to be the richest. Back then, I was equal parts of genius and utter stupidity, like most children.

My words yelled across the playground startled, impressed and confused everyone in the end. I laugh when the thought crosses my mind every now and then. I let loose with passion and confidence, supported from behind by two of my best men. I shouted, "I hate you. You're going to be poorer than me in the end. You're ugly, stupid and … and… and … have no friends. You should be locked in an asylum because, you're mentally retarded!"

My two lieutenants in unison, "YEAH!!"

I continued, "Our friendship is through! I'm done with you. I'm gonna be so rich and have a party and invite the whole entire world, but oh no, not you!! Consider your invitation to my mansion cancelled. Maybe, when I'm done, you can shine my shoes. You're gonna be buried in a cardboard box and I'm gonna be laid to rest in … my golden coffin with a view!!"

17

MIND THE GAP

We're all responsible for our current mess.
Faith was placed in charismatic scoundrels,
 Who promised to look out for the rest.
It was misplaced faith given to the unworthy.
The signs pointed to the obvious.
They were never going to share their prosperity.

We allowed the distance between rich and poor to increase.
The top percent live lavishly.
While the rest can only look on longingly.
Equality and equity are resigned to our periphery.
We forgot to mind the gap!

Deep inside we're supposed to be all good.
If that were true,
Why don't we do what we should?
Working for the common good is actually foreign to us.
From conception our focus was personal survival.
It's at our core until we return to the dust.

We're born and remain selfish.
Hopefully, we find others we can trust.
Consistently we're disappointed in those
We endowed with money, power and status.

They have more than enough.
Yet, they crave more still.
Sacrificing others for their personal gain,
Becomes an addictive pill.

Giving and sharing their riches,
Somehow, makes them feel like they have less.
It makes sense in a world,
Where more, means success.
However, as the rich become richer,
The economic divide creates civil unrest.

Paranoia and anxiety about losing wealth steadily increase.

Valuable possessions of the wealthy overflows.
It's like a superfluous royal banquet feast.
Neglecting the less fortunate leads total destruction.
Evil deeds won't be absolved by religious confession.

We're sold a lie that wealth will trickle down.
The needy will only be left with scraps, scattered on the ground.
It doesn't make sense to drink from a restrictive pipe.
Think of the frustration filling a cup from pipe that's slow.
Our thirst will never be quenched.
It's easily solved by opening a flow.

Imagine if we let even a little of our wealth flow.
We'd all get our fill without the need live on credit.
There'd be less looking to borrow.
The weight of debt would be lifted of many shoulders.
No one's calling pressuring to pay what you owe.
Debts would be kept low.

However, as the poor struggle to survive day to day,
The fortunate live in oblivious excess.
They are unaware of the system's decay.
Give a little, you get a little.
Give a lot, you receive a lot.
To fix the problem of the haves and have not,
All parts of the system working cohesively and efficiently,
Is the solution to solve societal rot.

18

THE WISE FOOL

You can always find the wise within the crowd.//
They won't be brash and bold.//
They won't be the ones shouting out loud.//
That is the action of a fool.//
Openly expressing only their point of view.//
They profess to have all the answers.//
They reinvent the old claiming it's new.//
The wise do not seek praise or accolades.//
Most of them prefer solitude.

Separation from the noise, allows the wise to reflect.//
They use their power to change what they can.//
What's out of their control they openly accept.//
Only a fool would think they can control all.//
Their ignorance is quickly revealed.//
Fools don't learn from each fall.

The wise will see failure as an opportunity.//
They know there's more to learn from defeat.//
The fool tries to learn only from victory.//
Wise individuals realize there's more to life than they know.//
It gives them a sense of peace.//
The fool always tries to put on a show.//
They are satisfied with what they've already learned.//
The wise consistently seeks ways to grow.

They realize learning is a continual process.

Its takes time and patience.

Fools rush into action.
They don't take the time to listen to their conscience.

Look how much the wise know and so much more.

The fool is ignorant to them all.

However, the wise realize they truly know nothing.

So, each and every one is truly a fool after all.

19

BE

Be like the trees in the wind.
They sway together in harmony.
Feel nature's magic weave over your skin.
Close your eyes and accept the feeling.
Let it penetrate deep within.

Be like the beasts basking in the sun.
They openly relax and absorb its rays.
Feel nature's energy that nourishes everyone.
Allow its pure power into your darkened soul.
Let it give you light when you have none.

Be like the creatures soaring in the sky.
They coast on uplifting thermals high above.
Feel daily stresses underneath pass by.
A bird's eye view helps keep a healthy distance.
Let worries and concerns live where they lie.

Be like the waves of the ocean.
They surf along a current without concern.
Feel nature's rhythm and ride its motion.
Rise and crash where you will.
Let the search for peace of mind be your devotion.

Value the moments that give mental release.
They offer opportunities for escape.

Seek out those simple pleasures.

Let them bring you some peace.

20

His inner monologue bore mental fruit. The experiences from his past were to be used to understand his fleeting present. That understanding could be a helpful guide, as the future was never that far away. The future was uncertain and ever changing. It was waiting for all who had life to see it. We had no control of it. This was due to the fact that there were too many variables to create a proper algorithm. What he thought he knew was actually irrelevant in the grand scheme. At the very least he knew that was needed to master living in his world, was beyond him and he was never to fully comprehend existence. There was never going to be enough time for him to find all the connections. However, he felt fortunate to be able to realize that trying to connect everything was a fruitless exercise. Life had taught him and others that is was the journey and not the destination that was paramount.

His journey was dependent on the journey of others, intentionally or otherwise. It was easy to get lost on the journey, with the numerous distractions. However, we were all gifted with the power of choice. No one had figured out the perfect life. All we can do is the live the miraculous life given to us, the best we think. There was no point complaining, because we were not alone in our struggles. Forever linked all life was, whether understood or not. Finally, he concluded that he was lucky enough to exist at some point in a living cycle that was both independent and dependent of him. He was satisfied with the course of his life. It was never supposed to be easy with unimaginable joy. There was only going to be a level of happiness equitable to suffering. Also, because of the universal connection, his body might have limits, but his connected spirit could never be shackled. The greater the connection, the stronger his spirit. Realizing that his spirit was an abstract energy, it could not be destroyed. Energy could only be transferred or transformed. There was an energy constantly moving around and through all of us, along an invisible thread.

AN INVISIBLE THREAD

We and all living things are connected.

We're linked by an invisible thread.

For many, it's not easily detected.

All actions, through the thread are felt.

It's part of a universal web, therefore, all are affected.

When we pull in our own direction,
Distance is created and there's less connection.

Access to the web's benefits becomes restricted.

There's no safety in numbers, which offers protection.

We begin to lose the value of our bind.

When you're most in need of help,

It'll be hard to find.

Naivety and arrogance allow you to think, you can survive on your own.
Everything is dependent on another.

No living thing exists alone.

One cannot be without others and vice versa.

We're linked through cycles of birth and finality.

It's like the beginning and ending of an era.

Each contributes to the life of each other.

The web's fibers allow us to be whole.

 Each contributes to the life all others.

Therefore, creating a shared connected soul.

We're like the leaves of a tree,
Or like roots below the surface.
Perpetually we play our part,
Fueling life's ultimate purpose.

EPILOGUE EPIPHANY

It had taken him a lifetime to realize and appreciate what he considered the most important connection. Connection, that powerful agent of influence went overlooked throughout his life. It didn't matter that it took him so long to come to that conclusion, because he was only in a race with himself. He was happy and content with the race he ran. The embers of his life's fires were approaching their dim conclusion, and he used what reserves of conscious power available to find summation of his journey. He was low on time for conscious thought and he wanted to rejoice during his transition from life to death. He was thankful and had no regrets. The epiphany of universal connection made him realize that he was never alone. There was truly no independence of living things, only denial of dependence. For, even though the final steps towards cessation appear to be taken according to individual design, they were dependent on the roads created by others and in association with the individual making the trek. That thought gave him comfort and contentment.

Although his revelations came at his life's latter stages, he was content because it was by design, like all things in his life. If it were his destiny to be privy to such insights earlier in his life, the life he remembered now would be mere fiction. The life he was afforded was a gift from a greater power than himself. Realizing that apparent truth gave him contentment, humility and some sense of clarity. He knew there was little point in trying to deceive the one individual who knew him the best, to his core, himself. What benefit would come from personal delusion, especially witnessing the many perils created from that state of mind? What was to be gained, especially at the conclusion of his life?

He was able to encapsulate the life he lived by comparing it to a hypothetical challenging situation. The conclusion from both scenarios would be the same. At the end of each, he would be happy because he was thankful, and content. This, he thought to be the logical and emotionally satisfying option. They would lead him on a path to the acceptance of the limits of his powers. He only had the power to influence, never did he have total control. The flow of his life would provide sufficient proof of powerlessness. His life was akin to being awoken suddenly, somewhere in a foreign jungle world, against is conscious will. The ultimate purpose was to secure a route for escape. This would have to be done in a fixed amount of time that he would never be made aware of.

During his life quest he was supposed to fall. The floor of life's jungle was a changing, precarious terrain. So, when he lost his balance, stumbled and slipped, there was ample strength to regain firm footing. From his initial introduction to that strange world, the only thing that was clear about his chosen route to find freedom was there were going to be a myriad of obstacles in his way. He was supposed to use his given gifts to overcome them. His initial introduction was a crippling, shocking barrage of light, sound and movement. He compared the assault on his senses to being in the epicenter of an epic, continual battle between an unknown number of warring factions in a dual natured jungle, savage and beautiful within the same breath. All around and about him where the echoes and pings of unyielding random shots fired in the jungle. The air was thick with trepidation and uncertainty. From as far back as he could remember that noise was rarely quieted.

It was a noise, which was the result of the unleashing of the arsenals of the jungle's combatants. They were no ordinary weapons and rarely was there a place to find refuge from them. Imagine trying to defend against impending incendiaries from cannons of control, biological weapons of buy and sell, tanks of truth, landmines of lies, bombs of beautiful and ugly to name a few of the chosen weapons used in the seemingly perpetual battle. The conflict was continually fueled by cumulative, combustible rhetoric aimed at multiple targets. All these were present in a jungle never at rest. It was a place of patterns and cycles securely fastened to boomerangs of beginning and end.

He would have no knowledge of anything helpful for survival in a world that he was equally ignorant about. He was born as a result of the seemingly inseparable union of mother nature and father time. He would arrive at a stage where his body was at its most feeble. So useless it would be that he wouldn't even be able to crawl. His body needed time to develop into its full maturity and his mind would require the same, if not more, time. Compounding the obvious issues of his forced odyssey, he would probably never know the true purpose of his existence.

However, the struggle for survival was a shared experience. There were others on their own mission in that unforgiving environment. So, because of this, he instantly learned that he was not the first to wake in the jungle of life. Life would also teach him that he wouldn't be the last either. All these factors combined to create an incredible amount of uncertainty. It would be a consistent theme throughout his life. He was thankful that eventually he would find the strength to accept the unceasing battles awaiting him as he navigated a world he was never going to master. Only the jungle's creator could conquer it. An honest conversation with his reflection in life's mirror gave a clear answer as to who was the greatest. The creator was the greatest of all and because of his lack of control, the one above all, beyond the jungle's perimeter, who reigned, wasn't him.

He was thankful that he didn't fall prey to the trappings of accumulating material things. He was content with the things he deemed important. He wasn't innocent of having attachments to things that time would prove were given superfluous significance. He was thankful that he was able to see that earthly attachments were part of a lineage beginning with labels placed on boxes residing on biased lists. The owner continually adds false value to the contents. So much so that separation from those precious items became extremely difficult and many were unable or unwilling to let go, creating a bond, an attachment. He was happy with the moments where he was able to realize that true value was found in purpose, not titles. It was a common error made by imperfect creatures.

Having less attachments proved to be a wise choice for his journey. He had less weight to carry while exploring the jungle. It afforded him a greater ability to range the world without a cumbersome load increasing the difficulty of an already arduous task. The jungle was constantly changing and he was thankful that he was able to see much of that world. Although he wasn't able to circumnavigate the whole world, he was content with where he was able to visit, the many interesting spaces of the jungle world.

During his wanderings under the jungle's canopy, he eventually realized that some answers he sought were given to him from the beginning. He was happy he was able to connect the lives of the birds, the bees and the creatures of the sea to his own. At times, he was able to bask in the sun's radiant energy and soar above the troubles that resided near or on the jungles floor, achieving some peace of mind. Although those moments weren't as much as he would've liked, he was content with his allocated time in those periodic rays of light, allowing him to fight the darkness of life's jungle. Those beams of joy provided much needed relief from the darkness, constantly try to rule his world.

Dangers and obstacles lurking in the shadows were difficult to detect. He took solace in the fact that he was eventually armed with a powerful weapon to defend himself, his logic. With logic by his side, he was able to use it to provide some clarity in the jungle's muddy waters of choice. It could be used to employ those lights of love, community, connection, peace, hope and grace amongst others, as guides in defense against the dark. They would aid in his escape by lighting the way and provide adequate shields against impending danger. Biding their time, were many formidable foes and forces, of which were such things like hate, jealousy, temptation and greed. Although there were many times he was lost in the darkness of life's jungle, he was happy and thankful that he was always able to find his way back to the light.

Although he was happy that he had suffered less than others, he was content with the strength gained from overcoming his suffering to gain increased patience and perseverance. For, the result of those personal battles seemed to shape his character more than those moments of personal success. The interval between his final breaths began to increase noticeably. His time was almost up. The jungle life analogy he created was similar to his condition, nearing conclusion. Somehow, he survived against all odds and now the jungle's darkness was beginning to give way to the light of salvation.

His journey in the jungle had provided so much. He was content with his total experience. The happiness one should feel at the moment of escape from that abstract jungle would be chosen as his final feelings while escaping life. There was never going to be a golden coffin awaiting him when he passed and he was content with that notion. However, he was even happier that he had no desire for one. What would be the purpose for such a thing, especially for a wise fool? There would be no point, like living a life based on irrational extremes, such as negative and positive and other illusions. They only served as distractions from his truth.

The truth was that during his lifetime and those of his ancestors, a prescription for a so-called perfect life hadn't been created. All that was ever created was merely biased opinion emanating from fallible creatures. Subjectivity claiming to be objectivity was further evidence of the contradictory, dual nature consistent of that jungle world where he had no choice to live out his days. Only by the development of his given gifts to differentiate between facts and fiction, would he be able to properly navigate the labyrinth of life's jungle. Time had proved that many labels and perceptions eventually change and few things were constant.

Change and time were two of the few constants in the jungle world. They were on a small list, which included death. Even though the reality of life after death was a mystery, it, like all constants wasn't to be feared. It was inevitable and a natural part of the jungle's existence. His body was required for the jungle's natural cycle of beginning and end. Beginning and end was like time and change, fueling the other's existence. One could not exist without the other. It was symbolic of the symbiotic relationship between the jungle and him.

This made him realize that even though his body's battle with time in the jungle was destined to fail, it would still serve a purpose even at the end. It made him happy to think of this. Although there were seemingly random shots fired in the jungle, he was content with how his mind and body served him. Some of those shots hit their mark creating slow healing wounds. A few, he was able to defend against. While others rarely, if ever, made contact and echoed in the distance. He was thankful that he was able to fight as long as he did. His soul, spirit, his energy would not disappear regardless of the outcome, which made him happy. For, energy cannot be destroyed and his would live on beyond the separation from his body, a bargain he was content to engage in. It was the only thing he could take with him to the other side, not his wife, children or any other perceived things of value. Therefore, there was no point having earthly attachments.

However, he was happy and content with the things and people he held close to his heart throughout his life. They played their part in his continued survival in the jungle. Although his mental reflections took him on an emotionally cathartic path laden with fluctuations of highs, lows and in-betweens, only happiness, thankfulness and contentment remained in the end. Oh, what a life he had lived with so many tales to tell. He was able to suppress the initial trepidations about survival in an unforgiving place, with feelings of confidence about his entire experience. His confidence stemmed from his ability to cultivate the courage and strength to untie himself from many of the jungle's burdens by fighting less and simply letting go. Somehow at his final moment, he was happy to follow that philosophy. The light of freedom beckoned and he wasn't about to resist. As he ventured forth towards the bright, he was content to release his hold to a precarious physical life, at the mercy of an unknown master, under the canopy of life's jungle. While exhaling his last breath, he thanked the creator and simply, let go.

Made in the USA
Middletown, DE
06 April 2019